BY TOM ANGLEBERGER

ILLUSTRATED BY CECE BELL

Amulet Books · New York

PUBLISHER'S NOTE: This is a work of fiction. Names, characters, places, and incidents are either the product of the author's imagination or are used fictitiously, and any resemblance to actual persons, living or dead, business establishments, events, or locales is entirely coincidental.

Library of Congress Cataloging-in-Publication Data

Angleberger, Tom, author.
Inspector Flytrap / by Tom Angleberger ; illustrated by Cece Bell.
pages cm
ISBN 978-1-4197-0948-7
[1. Mystery and detective stories. 2. Venus's flytrap—Fiction. 3. Goats—Fiction. 4. Animals—Fiction. 5. Humorous stories.] I. Bell, Cece, illustrator. II. Title.
[Fic]—dc23
2015016400

Hardcover ISBN: 978-1-4197-0948-7
Paperback ISBN: 978-1-4197-0965-4

Text copyright © 2016 Tom Angleberger
Illustrations copyright © 2016 Cece Bell
Book design by Maria T. Middleton

Printed and bound in U.S.A.
10 9 8 7 6 5 4 3 2

Amulet Books are available at special discounts when purchased in quantity for premiums and promotions as well as fundraising or educational use. Special editions can also be created to specification. For details, contact specialsales@abramsbooks.com or the address below.

**ABRAMS** The Art of Books
115 West 18th Street, New York, NY 10011
abramsbooks.com

For Dav and Sayuri Pilkey

# CONTENTS

# PART 1
............
# Inspector Flytrap
# in
# The Da Vinci
# Cold

# Chapter 1

**M**y phone rang.

"Hello," I said. "Fly-trap Detective Agency."

A slow voice started asking me questions.

"Is this Mr. Flytrap?"

"My name," I answered, "is *Inspector* Flytrap. I am a detective."

"Are you really a plant?"

"Yes, I am a Venus flytrap, a rare type of plant that catches and eats flies."

"Did you say flies?" the slow voice asked.

"Yes."

"You eat *flies*?"

"Yes. And any other small insects I can catch."

"That's disgusting!"

I was starting to get mad.

"Listen, pal," I said. "Look me up in the encyclopedia, if you want, but I don't have time to be slowly insulted all day. Do you have a mystery for me to solve or not?"

"Yes."

"Is it a BIG DEAL mystery?"

"Well . . . ," said the slow voice. "It is . . . a big deal . . . to me . . ."

"OK, pal," I said. "Tell me about it. As *quickly* as possible. I'm in a big hurry!"

"I lost my pickle paperweight."

"What's that?"

"It's a metal pickle . . . that's used to hold papers . . . down on a desk."

"Sorry, pal," I said. "I solve only BIG DEAL mysteries!"

And I hung up before he could start a slow argument about it.

Sheesh! A lost metal pickle! Who cares! That's a SMALL DEAL.

I'm trying to become the greatest detective that ever grew! I don't have time to go around looking for metal pickles!

Niha's NUTRITIOUS DIET!

# Chapter 2

**M**y phone rang.

"Hello," I said. "Flytrap Detective Agency."

A beautiful voice said, "Is this Mr. Flytrap?"

"Actually, it's *Inspector* Flytrap," I said. "Do you have a mystery?"

"Yes, I do," said the beautiful voice.

"Is it a BIG DEAL mystery?"

"Yes! It is a very, *very* BIG DEAL!"

The beautiful voice told me all about it. I said I would be right over.

After I hung up the phone, I shouted for my assistant, Nina the Goat. She's a goat.

"Nina! Get the skateboard! They've got a BIG DEAL mystery at the art museum!"

"Big deal," said Nina, who was busy gnawing on my desk. She is always hungry. And she eats everything—old shoes, tires, broccoli, and cans of spaghetti. By that I mean she eats the spaghetti *and* the can! It's scary to have an assistant who eats everything, especially for a plant like me.

But when she's not eating things and making me nervous, Nina is really helpful.

She helps me get around. See, I can't just walk down to the crime scene or run after a suspect. Like I said, I'm a plant. Plants don't walk or run. We just sit. But I don't like to sit in one place too long.

Nina puts my flowerpot on a skateboard. Then she pushes me wherever I need to go.

This time we were headed downtown to the art museum. It's always scary when Nina has to push me through traffic. She never wants to wait for the light to change or to cross at the corner. She just shoves me out into the street, right in front of speeding traffic!

She always wants to go down one-way streets the wrong way, but I've told her it's too dangerous. I'd get run over, for sure!

I also like to avoid hills. When we have to go up a hill, Nina complains a lot. And when we go down a hill, she jumps on the board and we go way, *way* too fast.

When we rolled up to the art museum, there was an emu waiting for us.

"What a beautiful emu," I said.

"Big deal," said Nina.

"Hello, Mr. Flytrap," said the emu. It was the same beautiful voice I had heard on the phone. "I am Lulu Emu."

"Hello, Lulu Emu. I am *Inspector* Flytrap, and this is Nina the Goat. We're ready to solve your BIG DEAL mystery."

"SHHHHHHHHHHHH! This is all top secret!" said Lulu Emu. "We can't let anyone hear about it. There could be spies around."

I looked, but all I saw was a sloth reading a newspaper. It didn't look like a suspicious sloth, but then I'm not sure what a sloth looks like when it's being suspicious.

"If you'll follow me, I'll take you to the Top Secret Art Lab," said Lulu Emu.

She started to push me into the museum. "We don't allow horned mammals in here," she said to Nina.

Nina's eyes turned red. She gave Lulu a very, *very* nasty look.

"Nina is my assistant," I said. "I cannot and will not work on your BIG DEAL mystery without her."

"Oh, all right," said Lulu Emu. "But she has to be on her best behavior."

"Big deal," snarled Nina, and she butted my skateboard with her horns. I knew she was mad, but why does she always have to take it out on me?

"Watch it, Nina!" I yelled as she sent

Oopsie Chick

Enigma II

me rolling wildly through the doors.

As I went zooming helplessly through the museum, I saw lots of beautiful art.

I saw a huge painting of a chicken standing on its head. And a statue of an elephant covered in zebra stripes. Over my head were huge plastic vampire teeth, dangling from wires. Was that supposed to be art?

Finally my skateboard slowed down

Large Tooths

Mona Spaghetti

and stopped in front of a painting of a lady eating spaghetti.

Lulu Emu and Nina caught up to me.

"Ah," said Lulu Emu. "This is a very famous painting. It's called *The Mona Spaghetti*."

"Big meal," said Nina. She was looking a little hungry.

"Er . . . we'd better get right to work," I told Lulu Emu.

She took a remote control from her pocket and typed in a bunch of numbers.

The remote beeped, and then the spaghetti painting beeped, and then it swung open like a door. Behind it we could see a secret room with lots of microscopes and computers and stuff.

"Welcome to our Top Secret Art Lab," said Lulu Emu.

Mona Spaghetti

# Chapter 3

nside the Top Secret Art Lab there were a bunch of art scientists working on paintings and statues.

Lulu Emu led us to a painting of a flower. It was the most beautiful flower I had ever seen. Being a plant, I know a thing or two about beautiful flowers! And this one was good-looking!

"Big deal," said Nina.

"Look!" said Lulu Emu. "We have just found this painting by Leonardo da Vinci."

"Who?" I asked.

"Leonardo da Vinci was a famous painter and inventor who lived a long time ago," said Lulu Emu.

"Did he always paint flowers?" I asked.

"No," said Lulu Emu. "He painted pretty

ladies, horses, a flying machine, and many other things. In fact, he also painted *The Mona Spaghetti*, which you just saw. But this painting is the only flower painting he ever made."

"It's very pretty," I said. "But what's the BIG DEAL mystery about it?"

"Well, we think that da Vinci left a secret message! Look!"

Lulu Emu pointed to the bottom of the painting.

There was a yellow blob down there.

"Big deal," said Nina.

I had to agree with Nina. Had Lulu Emu called me just to look at a yellow blob?

"That doesn't really seem like a BIG DEAL mystery to me," I said.

"But it *is* a big deal," replied Lulu Emu. "Leonardo da Vinci was one of the smartest people ever. He may have left this message to give us great wisdom—or maybe even the secret of life."

I looked at the yellow blob. I did not see wisdom. I did not see the secret of life. I saw only a yellow blob.

"Or," said Lulu Emu, "maybe it's the secret to finding a great treasure."

I got out my magnifying glass.

"Push me closer, Nina. I want a better look."

"You didn't say 'please,'" said Nina.

"OK, *please* push me closer."

She shoved my skateboard with a hoof, and I rolled over to the painting.

# Chapter 4

All the art scientists crowded around to see what I would see when I looked at the blob.

"Hmm," I said.

I said "Hmm" so it would sound like I was thinking something really smart.

Instead, I was thinking that I was looking at a yellow blob. A slightly greenish-yellow blob, actually.

Wait a minute! Maybe the blob looked like a hand . . . a pointing hand! Well, not really. Maybe the letter R? No, not much.

Or a duckie? Or Nina's mom?

No, not any of those things. It just looked like a blob.

"Have you had the blob scientifically tested?" I asked.

"No, it's too important and valuable for us to even touch," said Lulu Emu. "Hey! What's your goat doing?"

Nina was licking the yellow blob.

"Stop!" shouted Lulu Emu and all the scientists. "That blob is priceless!"

"Big deal," said Nina. "It's too salty anyway."

"Salty?" I said. "Hmm."

This time I said "Hmm" because I really meant it.

Finally it was starting to make sense. I just needed to know one more thing.

"Do you know anything about Leonardo da Vinci?" I asked Lulu Emu.

"Of course! He was born in Italy in—"

I interrupted her. "Do you happen to know how tall he was?"

"About this tall," said Lulu Emu. She held out one foot just above the yellow blob.

"AHA!" I shouted. "I have solved the BIG DEAL mystery."

# Chapter 5

Lulu Emu and the art scientists were very excited. One of them got out a video camera.

"This is a BIG DEAL moment in the history of art," said Lulu Emu. "Please tell us what Leonardo da Vinci's mysterious yellow blob means."

"Imagine da Vinci in his studio," I said. "He has decided to paint a flower for the first time. He has never painted a flower before. He has a flower model to paint from. He does not realize that he is allergic to flowers.

"He has to sneeze! But his hands are full. He has a paintbrush in one hand. He has a paint tray in the other hand. He can't get out his hankie!

"AH-CHOO! He sneezes right on the painting."

"You mean," said Lulu Emu, "the yellow blob is a . . ."

"Yes," I said. "It is Leonardo da Vinci's booger!"

Lulu Emu groaned. The video camera was turned off. All of the art scientists grumbled and went back to their work.

Except for one, who seemed very excited.

"I'm in charge of the museum's Gallery of Mucus," he said, picking the yellow blob off the painting. "This will be our second-greatest exhibit, next to George Washington's earwax!"

Lulu Emu looked sad. A tear rolled down her beautiful feathery face.

"I'm sorry—" I started to say, but Nina gave me a hard push out the door.

DA VINCI'S SNOT     WASHINGTON'S EARWAX

# Chapter 6

Nina pushed me back through traffic to my office. I almost got run over by a minivan this time.

"Whew," I said when we reached the office. "I could really use a drink."

Nina poured a whole bottle of water into my pot. Then she ate the bottle.

"Ah, much better," I said. I was just starting to relax when my phone rang.

"Flytrap Detective Agency," I said. "Do you have a BIG DEAL mystery?"

"Yes," a beautiful voice said. "This is Lulu Emu. We have another BIG DEAL mystery at the art museum!"

"Already? What is it?"

"Someone has destroyed our most famous piece of art!"

"Which one was it?" I asked. "The upside-down chicken?"

"No," said Lulu Emu. "It's *The Mona Spaghetti*. It's got a big hole in it where the spaghetti used to be."

"AHA!" I shouted. "I have solved another BIG DEAL mystery."

"Already?" said Lulu. "Who did it?"

"It was my assistant, Nina the Goat. She took a bite out of the painting as we left."

Lulu Emu screamed. Her voice didn't sound so beautiful anymore.

"She's pretty mad, Nina," I said. "She says that painting was worth 100 million dollars."

"Big deal," said Nina.

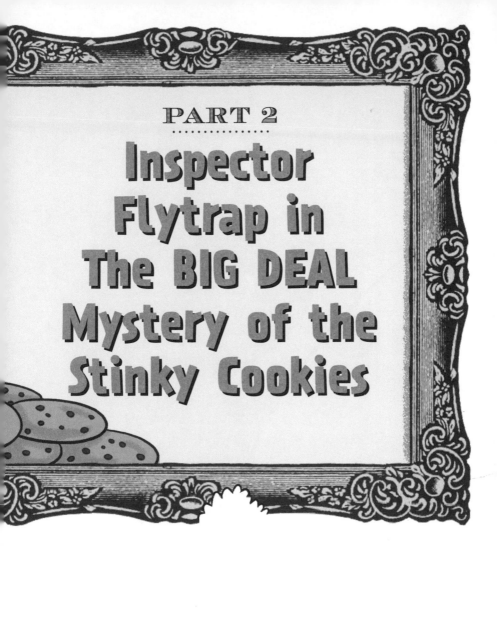

# PART 2

# Inspector Flytrap in The BIG DEAL Mystery of the Stinky Cookies

# Chapter 7

**M**y phone rang.

"Hello," I said. "Flytrap Detective Agency. Do you have a BIG DEAL mystery?"

A tiny voice said, "Yez-zzzzz."

"Are you a fly?" I asked.

"Yezzzzzzz," said the tiny voice.

"Sorry," I said. "I cannot work for flies. Sometimes I accidentally eat them."

The fly hung up.

# Chapter 8

**M**y phone rang.

"Hello," I said. "Flytrap Detective Agency. Do you have a BIG DEAL mystery?"

"You'd better believe it's a BIG DEAL, Mr. Flytrap!" said a crazy voice. "Are you kidding me? It's big, all right! It sure ain't small, I'll tell you that!"

"My name is *Inspector* Flytrap!" I said.

"If your mystery is really that big, maybe I should come over and see it for myself."

"See it? Flytrap, you need to come down here to Koko Dodo's Cookie Shop and *smell* it! Take one whiff and you won't have to ask if it's a BIG DEAL!"

This guy really is crazy, I thought, but he did seem to have a BIG DEAL mystery. I decided to take the case.

"Nina, get the skateboard," I said. "There's a BIG DEAL mystery down at Koko Dodo's Cookie Shop!"

"Big deal," said Nina. But I think she was secretly excited. She loves cookies.

The cookie shop was all the way across town, so Nina pushed me to the subway. I hate taking the subway because I'm afraid of getting stepped on. When you're a plant, getting stepped on isn't a joke. Luckily, I found a seat next to a sloth reading a newspaper. He never moved.

As soon as we got out of the subway, I noticed a strange smell.

"That doesn't smell like fresh-baked cookies," I told Nina.

Nina pushed me down the street to the cookie store. The smell got worse and

worse. A dodo was waiting for us out front.

"I'm Koko Dodo," said the dodo.

"My name is—," I began, but Koko Dodo kept right on talking.

"Do you smell that? That smells like a BIG DEAL, doesn't it? Huh? Yeah, yeah, it does!"

I wanted to hold my nose, but I don't have one.

"Is that smell coming from inside your cookie store?" I asked.

"How dare you!" snarled Koko Dodo. "The only smell that comes from inside my shop is from freshly baked cookies made using super-secret recipes from my great-great-great-grandpop's super-secret cookbook! I have super-secret recipes for over 300 different kinds of cookies, and they all smell good."

"Do you have a super-secret recipe for cookies with dead flies in them?" I asked.

"Of course not!" shouted Koko Dodo.

"Too bad," I said. "OK, if the smell isn't coming from inside your store, then where is it coming from?"

"From up there! On the roof!"

I looked at the roof. There was a very big shoe up there. It was as big as a bathtub.

"Big heel," said Nina.

# Chapter 9

Where did it come from?" I asked Koko Dodo.

"I have no idea! That's the BIG DEAL mystery! That's why I called you. *You're* supposed to figure it out."

"Well," I said, "it's big and it's a mystery, but why is it a BIG DEAL?"

"Why is it a BIG DEAL? Just look at my store!" said Koko Dodo.

I looked at it. It was empty. Well, except for the cookies. I mean, it was empty of customers.

"Usually I have customers lined up around the block! Now nobody will go in the store because they think my cookies stink," he fumed. "That's why I need you to solve the mystery—instead of just standing around asking questions all day!"

"Well, asking questions is how I usually solve a mystery," I told him. "But if it will make you feel better, I'll send Nina up there to taste the shoe."

"Why the heck would you do that?" Koko Dodo asked.

"Well, it worked the last time," I said. "Go ahead, Nina."

Most goats can jump very high. Nina can jump higher than most goats. She made a big jump and landed on the roof of the cookie store.

She took a great big bite out of the shoe. She chewed it for a minute, then started to turn green.

"ACK!" she bleated, and then she keeled over. She fell right off the roof. Luckily, she landed on Koko Dodo and was not injured.

"What did it taste like?" I asked when she had finished gagging and choking.

"Old fish," said Nina.

"And the beach.

"Rope.

"Boats.

I was not included

"Treasure chests.

"The Seven Seas."

She stopped and thought for a second.

"And dirty feet," she added.

"That's ridiculous," said Koko Dodo, still lying under Nina. "How would a goat know what dirty feet taste like?"

"You don't want to know," I told him.

# Chapter 10

This was a tough case!

Why was there only one shoe? Why was it so big? Why did it taste like old fish, the beach, rope, boats, treasure chests, the Seven Seas, and dirty feet?

Suddenly I knew the answer!

"AHA!" I shouted. "I have solved another BIG DEAL mystery!"

"Do you know whose shoe this is?" asked Koko Dodo.

"Yes! It belongs to a pegleg pirate."

"What's a pegleg pirate?" asked Koko Dodo.

"A pegleg pirate is a pirate who has lost a leg. Maybe a shark ate the leg, or maybe a cannonball hit it. So he has one real leg and one wooden leg. He only needs one shoe."

"But why a big shoe?"

"Because he's a *giant* pegleg pirate."

At this point, I expected Koko Dodo to thank me. He didn't.

TURN PAGE FOR A WHALE OF A TALE COMIC

"A giant pegleg pirate? That's all you've got? That's your solution? What I want to know is what to do about it!"

"Ah," I said. "That is a different BIG DEAL mystery."

"Can you solve it?"

"Not right now," I said. "We have to go."

"Why?"

"Because Nina is eating your great-great-great-grandpop's super-secret cookbook."

By the time Koko Dodo got to her, she was swallowing the last page.

Koko Dodo went nuts. He ran around in a circle flapping his tiny wings.

"I'm ruined! Ruined! I can't bake cookies without my super-secret recipes!"

We left quickly.

# Chapter 11

When we got back to the office, I decided to give Nina a lecture about not eating stuff that doesn't belong to her.

"Nina, you really upset Koko Dodo."

"Mmmrr mmrwlll," she said.

"What? I can't understand you when you talk with your mouth full."

She swallowed the doorknob that she had been chewing and said, "Big deal."

I was about to tell her that it really *was* a big deal when the phone rang.

"Flytrap Detective Agency," I said. "Do you have a mystery?"

A big voice said, "ARRRR! YES, MATEY!"

"Is it a BIG DEAL mystery?" I asked.

The big voice said, "ARRRRRR! YES, MATEY!"

"Are you a giant pegleg pirate who's missing a shoe?" I asked.

The big voice said, "ARRRR! YES, MATEY!"

"AHA! Another BIG DEAL mystery solved! You will find your shoe on top of Koko Dodo's cookie store downtown."

The big voice said, "ARRRR! THANKS, MATEY!"

# PART 3
· · · · · · · · · · · · · · ·
# Inspector Flytrap
# Has Lunch

# Chapter 12

L et's celebrate solving our latest BIG DEAL mystery," I said to Nina. "Let's go out for lunch."

Nina did not say "Big deal." She takes lunch very seriously. She doesn't care where we go—she just wants to go.

"How about Penguini's Linguini?" I asked. It's where we first met, when I was a table decoration with a dream and

Nina was dining alone . . . on the table-cloth.

Instead of answering, she pushed me out the door, and away we went. Luckily, Penguini's Linguini is on our block, so we didn't have to cross the street.

"Hey, Penguini!" I called as Nina pushed me through the front door.

"Hey, Inspector Flytrap! Great to see you again! Nina the Goat, you're looking good, honey!" I like Penguini because he always gets my name right.

"What was yesterday's special?" I asked.

"Anchovy ravioli," he said.

"Wonderful!" I said. "That works."

"Help yourselves!" said Penguini.

Nina pushed me right through the restaurant, past the kitchen, and into the alley in back.

There it was . . . an overloaded trash can filled with old, rotting food.

"Mmm," said Nina.

Above the trash can buzzed a cloud of flies.

"Mmm," I said.

We both had a feast.

# Chapter 13

**M**y phone didn't ring.

"Hey, Nina," I said. "I wonder why we're not getting any phone calls about BIG DEAL mysteries."

She didn't answer. She was busy chewing on something.

"Maybe there are no more BIG DEAL mysteries," I said.

Nina just kept chewing.

"Hey, maybe *that's* a BIG DEAL mystery!" I said. "The Mystery . . . of No More Mysteries! What do you think?"

Nina just kept on chewing.

"Hey, what are you eating over there?" I asked.

"Phone," she said.

"The phone!?! No wonder we're not getting any phone calls, Nina! You're ruining the Flytrap Detective Agency!"

"Big deal," said Nina.

"Well, it's a big deal to me. Quick, push me to the phone store!"

When we got to the phone store, the salesperson showed me the newest kind of phone. It was very, *very* small and had lots of neat extras, like a camera, electronic maps, and a high-powered 3-D video magnifying glass.

"Wow!" I said. "That would be perfect for my job as a detective. What do you think, Nina?"

She ate it in one bite.

"Too small," she said.

"Do you have any goat-proof phones?" I asked the salesperson. He showed me to the goat-proof-phone aisle. All the goat-

proof phones were big and clunky and didn't have cameras or any other cool stuff.

"All right," I said. "I guess I'll take the biggest, clunkiest, least cool phone you've got."

Back at the office, I plugged in the enormous new phone.

It rang right away!

"Flytrap Detective Agency. Do you have a mystery?"

A grumpy voice said, "Yeah, Mr. Flytrap, I sure do!"

"Actually, my name is *Inspector* Flytrap," I said.

"Who cares! All I care about is getting somebody to solve this mystery."

"Is it a BIG DEAL mystery?"

"Duh! Of course it is." said the grumpy voice. "I wouldn't waste my time calling you over a SMALL deal mystery."

The grumpy voice told me all about it.

"I'll be right over," I said and hung up the phone.

"Nina, will you please push me to Snooty la Tooty Gardens? Someone has stolen their largest and most beautiful flower."

"Big daffodil," said Nina.

"No," I said. "It's a rose."

# Chapter 14

'd never been to Snooty la Tooty Gardens before.

That's because it makes me sad to see plants locked up behind fences. I believe that all plants should be free to go wherever they want. But the truth is that I've never met another plant that actually wanted to go anywhere. Most plants are happy just to sit where they are.

But when Nina pushed me across Garden Street right in front of a speeding fire truck, I started to wish that I had stayed at home, too. The fire truck swerved just in time and we barely made it across alive.

There, waiting in front of the gates of Snooty la Tooty Gardens, was a really grumpy rat.

"I know what you're thinking, Mr. Flytrap! Well, I'm not a rat. I'm a kiwi. Mimi Kiwi."

"Hello, Mimi Kiwi," I said. "I am *Inspector* Flytrap, and this is Nina. I'm sorry I thought you were a rat."

"Hmmph," said the really grumpy kiwi.

"What's a kiwi?" I asked.

"DUH!" said Mimi Kiwi. "I am."

"Oh," I said.

There was an awkward silence. Finally I said, "Would you like to show me the scene of the crime?"

Mimi Kiwi muttered something and led us through the gate, down a path, and into a greenhouse.

The greenhouse was crammed with every kind of plant. They were all in pots, just like mine.

Mimi Kiwi pointed to an empty spot near the door.

"Is that where the rose was?" I asked.

"Duh!"

I guessed that she meant "Yes."

"So, was the missing rose in a pot?" I asked.

"Duh!"

"And the pot is missing, too?"

"Duh!"

I have to admit that I've never met an

animal—or a plant, for that matter—as rude and unhelpful as Mimi Kiwi. Even Nina seemed polite next to her. I gave up asking her questions and started looking around.

I found a tiny little clump of black stuff on the floor.

"Nina, would you mind eating this?" I asked.

Nina didn't mind.

"What's it taste like?" I asked.

"Potting soil," said Nina.

"Just as I suspected! The thief must have spilled some of the dirt when they moved the pot."

"Duh!" said Mimi Kiwi.

"Big deal," said Nina.

I ignored Mimi Kiwi, but I answered Nina.

"Actually, it's quite important. Notice that there are several other clumps of potting soil," I said. "It's like a trail of soil. And it goes right out the door."

"D—," Mimi Kiwi started to say, but we didn't stick around to hear her finish.

"Quick, Nina. Follow that dirt!" I cried, and she pushed me right out the door.

# Chapter 15

**N**ina and I followed the dirt out of Snooty la Tooty Gardens, down the street, around the corner, and up a long hill.

Nina complained and grumbled the whole way.

Finally, at the top of the hill, the dirt trail led us into a big park. And then I saw what we were after . . . a beautiful rose

. . . in a pot . . . on a skateboard . . . being pushed by a goat!

"AHA!" I shouted. "I have solved another BIG DEAL mystery!"

The other goat must have heard me, because suddenly it started pushing the rose really fast.

"Quick, Nina, after them!" I shouted.

The chase was on! The other goat was faster, but Nina was more daring and reckless. We gained ground by racing at full speed over big bumps, taking turns without slowing down, and weaving in between the feet of passing animals.

Sure, I was worried about crashing, but I didn't ask Nina to slow down. My potting soil was spilling out, too, but I didn't care. To solve the mystery I had to catch that flower!

Suddenly the flower slowed down and swerved onto the grass to go around some concrete steps.

I closed my eyes. I knew what Nina was about to do and I just couldn't look. She hopped on behind me and we went flying over the steps.

"Yee-haaaaaaaaaaaaaaaa!" shouted Nina.

We went right over a sloth sitting on the steps reading a newspaper.

When we hit the ground, I bounced and almost spilled. But somehow I stayed on the skateboard and we kept going. We were catching up to them.

But now we were on a long straight section of sidewalk. The other goat was just too fast. Nina got off and started pushing again, but we were falling behind. The rose was getting away.

I looked ahead and saw that the rose was about to run into some sort of lumpy metal thing that was on the sidewalk.

"Look out!" I shouted. "You're going to crash!"

But it was too late. The rose's skateboard hit the metal lump, the skateboard flipped over, and the rose tumbled off.

Nina had to use all four hooves as brakes to stop us just before we hit the metal lump, too. Now I could see that it was in the shape of a pickle. It was a pickle paperweight that someone had dropped in the park.

"AHA!" I shouted. "I have just solved two BIG DEAL mysteries at the same time!"

# Chapter 16

Nina pushed me over to where the rose lay on the sidewalk.

"We've got it now!" I shouted victoriously.

The rose straightened up and brushed itself off.

"I am not an 'it,'" said the rose. "I am a 'she.' My name is Wanda."

"Oh," I said. I felt like a real jerk. "I'm

sorry. I did not expect a talking rose."

"I did not expect a talking Venus fly-trap," said Wanda.

Then we took a good look at each other. "WOWZER!" I thought, "That is one beautiful plant! Her leaves! Her petals! Her stem! Her beautiful rosy eyes!"

"I did not expect such a beautiful rose," I said.

"And I did not expect such a handsome Venus flytrap," said Wanda.

It was love at first sight!

"Please do not take me back to the greenhouse," said Wanda. "I want to be free."

I did not expect that, either.

"You mean, you don't want to go back

to Snooty la Tooty Gardens?" I asked. "I thought you were being kidnapped."

"No! I was trying to escape from that awful place! This really nice goat was trying to help me."

"Hi! My name is William," said the goat.

"Hello, William, my name is Inspector Flytrap, and this is my assistant, Nina the Goat."

William looked at Nina.

"I did not expect such a beautiful goat," he said to Nina.

I expected Nina to say "Big deal," but she did not.

She said, "William, you are the goat I have dreamed of all my life. Let me kiss you! Kissy-kissy smooch-smooch!"

And then she kissed him. I did not expect that, and I don't think William did, either.

I was wondering if Wanda might give me a kiss, too, when I heard a roaring motor. A big pickup truck screeched to a halt in the street next to the park.

"Oh no!" cried Wanda. "It's Mimi Kiwi!"

"Duh!" said Mimi Kiwi, looking out of the window at us. "Put the rose in the truck, Flytrap."

"Are you going to take me back to the greenhouse?" asked Wanda.

"Duh!" said Mimi Kiwi.

Wanda looked at me with tears in her beautiful rosy eyes. "I want to stay with you!"

I turned to Mimi Kiwi.

"Mimi, I love this rose. I will not help you take her back to the greenhouse."

Then I turned to the goats.

"Nina! William! Will you help us escape?"

Nina and William got Wanda's pot back on her skateboard. I picked up the pickle paperweight.

"Let's go!" I hollered.

"Wait!" shouted Mimi Kiwi. "If I don't get the rose back, then you didn't really solve the mystery."

"Big deal," I said.

# Chapter 17

We took off, zooming down the sidewalk as fast as Nina and William could go.

I heard the squeal of tires and knew that Mimi Kiwi was right behind us.

I looked back to see if she was gaining on us and saw something even worse.

It was Lulu Emu! She was driving a bus full of art scientists. They were all leaning out of the windows and shouting and hollering at us.

"You've got to pay for that painting, Mr. Flytrap!" Lulu Emu screamed.

But I could barely hear her, because a motorcycle was racing up behind her. Koko Dodo was driving it!

"Mr. Flytrap, you ruined my business!" Koko Dodo was shouting.

"ARRRRR! AND YOU RUINED MY SHOE, MR. FLYTRAP!" came a big booming voice from behind him. It was a giant pegleg pirate on a rollerskate!

Last of all came a sloth with a newspaper riding an old-timey bicycle.

"You keep bugging me

while I'm trying to read the paper, Mr. Fly-trap!" the sloth yelled.

"My name," I yelled back at all of them, "is *Inspector* Flytrap!"

# Chapter 18

**H**ow can we ever escape?" I cried. "They're too fast!"

"Big hill," said Nina, turning my skateboard so we went down a side street. William and Wanda did the same.

I looked ahead. It was the steepest hill in the whole city.

"NO, NINA!" I shouted, but it was too late. She hopped on my skateboard, and

William hopped on Wanda's. I felt gravity take over, pulling us down, down, down. Faster and faster!

Just before we started to plunge down the hill I saw a street sign. It said ONE WAY. And it was pointing the other way!

A huge busload of ostriches was coming right at us.

"Duck!" yelled Wanda.

"No, ostriches," I said.

"NO! DUCK!"

We both got our heads down just in time as Nina and William steered us under the bus. A huge tire roared by, just inches from my pot.

STOP OR ELSE

ONE W

"Big wheel," said Nina.

We came out from under the bus and saw a whole fleet of taxis coming up the hill right at us. The taxi drivers honked and yelled. We dodged and swerved. A taxi's bumper bumped my pot, but Nina kept me from falling off.

We barely squeaked between the last two taxis. We shot out into an empty lane. There was open road ahead of us, which was good since we were now speeding out of control!

I looked back and saw Lulu Emu's bus, Koko Dodo's motorcycle, Mimi Kiwi's pickup truck, and the sloth's bicycle all stuck in a huge traffic jam. The giant peg-

leg pirate had bumped his shin on the ostrich bus and was sitting on the ground, crying like a baby.

"Look out!" yelled Wanda.

I turned around. "Look out!" I screamed.

The street was ending. We were going so fast we couldn't stop. We were headed straight for a restaurant.

It was Penguini's Linguini.

"Do you have a cell phone?" I asked Wanda.

"Here you go," she said, handing it to me.

I dialed the number and waited.

"We're going to crash!" yelled Wanda.

Penguini answered the phone.

"Hello, Penguini's Linguini. Today's special is—"

"HEY, PENGUINI! OPEN THE DOOR!" I yelled.

The door swung open and we zoomed through. Penguini called,

"Hey, Inspector Flytrap! Nina, you're looking good! I see you brought friends."

We crashed into his kitchen. Pots and
pans and goats and skateboards and
linguini went everywhere.

# Chapter 19

**B**y the time Wanda and I had recovered, the goats were already eating the pots, the pans, and the linguini.

"Hey, Penguini," I said. "Please bring us two bottles of your finest sparkling water. We have a lot to celebrate."

Penguini popped the corks and poured the fizzy water into our pots. Ahh . . .

I took Wanda's leaf, being careful of her thorns, and gazed into her beautiful rosy eyes.

And we lived happily ever after.

# ACKNOWLEDGMENTS

The title of Part 1, "Inspector Flytrap in the Da Vinci Cold" is a parody of a famous adult book, *The Da Vinci Code*, which I have not read. Some books that I *have* read, though, are by Daniel Pinkwater. Pinkwater is very funny and writes about pickles, which inspired me to try to be very funny and write about pickles.

I would also like to acknowledge some goats I have known: Spooky, Skippy, and Jimmy. I have seen Venus flytraps in person, but we've never become friends.

And I'd really like to thank Cece Bell for working so hard to illustrate these books!

You wouldn't believe the amount of research she did. If I wrote that Nina the Goat ate a shoe, then Cece would actually eat a shoe herself! Now *that's* an artist!

—Tom

Thanks to the amazing Tom for writing the words, to the magnificent Susan Van Metre for her sharp editing, to the übertalented Maria Middleton and Chad Beckerman for illustration guidance, and to the genius Kyle T. Webster, whose super-cool Photoshop brushes helped me complete my drawings.

No Venus flytraps or goats were harmed as I created the illustrations; as they were *completely made up*. Seriously.

—Cece

# ABOUT THE AUTHOR

**TOM ANGLEBERGER** is the author of the best-selling Origami Yoda series, as well as *Fake Mustache* and *Horton Halfpott*, both Edgar Award nominees, and The Qwikpick Papers series. Visit Tom online at origamiyoda.com.

# ABOUT THE ILLUSTRATOR

**CECE BELL** is the author of the *New York Times* bestselling *El Deafo*, which won a Newbery Honor. She is also the author of *The Rabbit and Robot* books. Tom and Cece are married and live in Christiansburg, Virginia.